To rescue dogs everywhere.
And to the lucky people who take them
into their hearts and homes—ESP

For Dani, with all my love—LM

PENGUIN YOUNG READERS
An Imprint of Penguin Random House LLC, New York

Penguin supports copyright. Copyright fuels creativity, encourages diverse voices, promotes free speech, and creates a vibrant culture. Thank you for buying an authorized edition of this book and for complying with copyright laws by not reproducing, scanning, or distributing any part of it in any form without permission. You are supporting writers and allowing Penguin to continue to publish books for every reader.

The publisher does not have any control over and does not assume any responsibility for author or third-party websites or their content.

Text copyright © 2020 by Erica S. Perl.
Illustrations copyright © 2020 by Penguin Random House LLC. All rights reserved.
Published by Penguin Young Readers, an imprint of Penguin Random House LLC, New York.
Manufactured in China.

Visit us online at www.penguinrandomhouse.com.

Library of Congress Cataloging-in-Publication Data is available upon request.

ISBN 9781524793418 (pbk)   10 9 8 7 6 5 4 3 2 1
ISBN 9781524793425 (hc)   10 9 8 7 6 5 4 3 2 1

The Lucky Dogs

Penny and Clover, Up and Over

by Erica S. Perl
illustrated by Leire Martín

Come on, Penny.

Come on, Clover.

Jump like me.

Jump up and over.

Good dog, Penny.

Come on, Clover.

Jump like Penny.

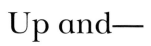

Up and—

Clover.

14

15

No.

Not that way.

Come on, Clover.

You can do it.

Up and over.

Up.

Up.

Up.

Up and—

Over.

Clover did it.